Robert Ellice Mack

All Round the Clock

Robert Ellice Mack

All Round the Clock

ISBN/EAN: 9783337395346

Printed in Europe, USA, Canada, Australia, Japan

Cover: Foto ©Andreas Hilbeck / pixelio.de

More available books at **www.hansebooks.com**

All round
the Clock

by
Robert Ellice Mack

Illustrated
by
Harriett M. Bennett.

London
Ernest Nister

Printed in Bavaria
783

New York
E. P. Dutton & Cº

ALL THE WAY
ROUND THE CLOCK.

*W*HEN clouds cover the sun's bright ray,
When rain-drops patter where we play,
It is a long, long toilsome way
All the way round the Clock.

When Master Fred can't do his sums,
Or lesson pages marked with thumbs,
The hours seem years till bedtime comes,
All the way round the Clock.

When deep down in the churchyard grey,
We laid our baby yesterday,
It seemed a thorn-set, weary way,
All the way round the Clock.

When daisy-stars come out with Spring,
And cowslips home the children bring,
Like larks at morn, the children sing,
All the way round the Clock.

When in the nursery firelight they
Whisper sweet tales, the children say:
"What pity 'tis so short a day,"—
All the way round the Clock!

Contents

T DAYBREAK.

BREAK slowly, softly, happy Day,
    For daybreak is so sweet;
O gently flowing River, stay
    Your silvern tripping feet;
O white, white Swan, your slumber keep,
My Little One lies fast asleep.

AN INVITATION.

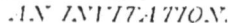

GIRLS and boys,
  Come out to play;
The sun is shining
  Away, away!

Into the meadow
  Over the way,
Tumbling and tossing
  The new-mown hay.

Into the hedgerow,
  Picking the may;
Over the hills
  And far away.

Down by the brook,
  Where the
    ripples play,
  Whirling and winding
    Their silvery way.

Wider and wider,
  Until they lay
In the peaceful breast
  Of the far-off bay.

Then home again
  By a different way,
Picking an armful
  Of wild-flowers gay

For Mother dear,
  To gladden her way
And wake in her heart
  A cheerful lay.

For every leaf
  Has its sunny ray,
All nature is happy,
  And seems to say:

"Girls and boys,
  Come out to play;
The sun is shining—
  Away, away!"

OUT
OF
REACH.

_D_OWN in a little shady spot
  A wild rose briar grew.
Said Dick: "I'll pluck it, Mary dear,
  And it shall be for you."
He soon found out 'twas out of reach
  And gave up with a sigh;
Said he: "When we are taller,
  We'll reach it by-and-by."

Now he's a man and she's a maid,
  Down where the briar grew;
He woo'd her, saying: "Mary dear,
  I'll win the world for you.
And you shall be its Queen, my dear,
  For ever and for aye;
Such dreams are out of reach just now;
  We'll reach them, though, some day."

A little Mary came to them
  Just when the roses blew;
And when the roses faded
  Their rosebud faded too.
"Sweet wife," said he, "our child's in heaven;
  Nay, nay, you must not cry
That she is far beyond our reach,
  Beyond the far blue sky;
Please God we'll meet our child in heaven,
  We'll meet her by-and-by."

A DISAPPOINTMENT.

*S*IPPITY, sippity, sop!
    I fear that you've
        drunk every drop.
  Said Fido: "I think
    You might leave me a drink,
Drippety, drippety, drop!"

Mippety, mippety, mop!
Said the cat: "He never will stop;
  The milk and the bread
  Will fly to his head,
Pippety, pippety, pop!"

Sippity, sippity, sop!
Drained to the last little drop.
  Said Fido: "I own
  I'd rather a bone
Than the very best basin of sop,
Hoppety, hoppety, hop."

SORROWS.

HOW shall I sing, little Maidie?
    Sing when your tears are wet.
Sorrow is sweet, little Maidie;
    Pity your poor little pet.
  This the only song I sing:
  There's pain and joy in everything.

But there is One, little Maidie,
    Knows your sorrow and grief,
Cares for the poor little sparrows,
    He soon will send you relief.
      Life's no plaything, no new toy,
      It brings to every girl and boy
      Rain and sunshine, sorrow, joy;
      This the only song I sing:
      There's pain and joy in everything.

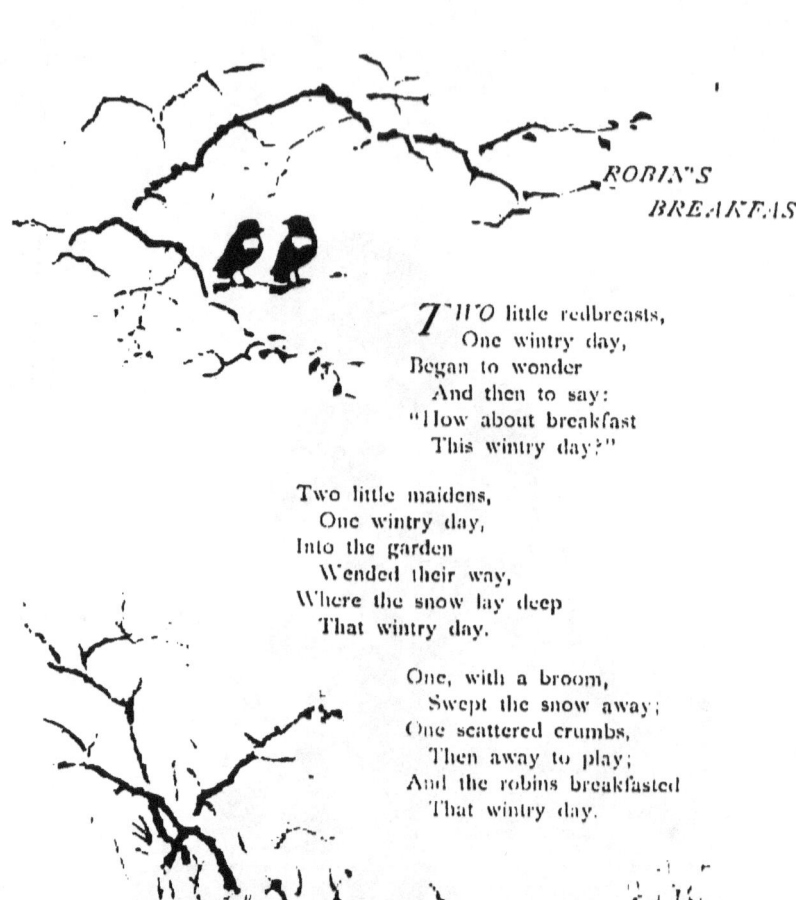

ROBIN'S
BREAKFAST.

TWO little redbreasts,
  One wintry day,
Began to wonder
  And then to say:
"How about breakfast
  This wintry day?"

Two little maidens,
  One wintry day,
Into the garden
  Wended their way,
Where the snow lay deep
  That wintry day.

One, with a broom,
  Swept the snow away;
One scattered crumbs,
  Then away to play;
And the robins breakfasted
  That wintry day.

A DARING ENTERPRISE.

TWO little folk, one Summer day,
    Were walking hand in hand,
And soon a daring enterprise
    These two brave hearts had planned:
It was to stop the rising tide
    From coming on the sand.

Now, Ben, he had a bucket,
    And Sissy had a spade;
And first they heaped a lot of stones —
    Foundations must be laid —
And long before the sun had set,
    A splendid fort was made.

"Now that's the sort of fort," said Ben,
    "Where you and I can hide;
The sea won't come along the sand,
    For we shall stop the tide."
At that a wicked little wave
    Laughed as it licked the side.

It laughed until it broke in two,
    And ran back down the shore;
"There now," said Ben, "I told you so:
    It won't come any more;"
When back there came upon his ear
    The sea's deep sullen roar.

Then louder roared the angry tide,
    And higher rose the sea,
Till by-and-by there came a wave
    As big as any three,
And stormed the fort and garrison
    As clean as clean could be.

The sun smiled sadly as he set,
    Whilst homeward, hand in hand,
Went two unhappy victims
    Of an enterprise they'd planned:
Which was, to stop the rising tide
    From coming on the sand.

KEPT IN.

I ASKED him why he was "kept in";
  "It's just this way," he said:
"It's not that I don't know my books—
  They won't stay in my head.

"I have to think of lots of things—
  My donkey, poor old Ned,
Also the money-box I keep
  Close underneath my bed,
And then my lessons all at once
  Slip right out of my head.

"And I know of a robin's nest,
  That's built behind the shed;
I feed the robins every day--
  The mother bird has fled.
I only wish these lessons
  Would just stop in my head."

And then a tear rolled down his cheek,
  His cheek so round and red,
And then the little fellow gave
  A quiet sob, and said:
"It's not that I don't know my books -
  They won't stay in my head."

A HEAVY WASH.

THIS is the way we wash the clothes,
    we wash the clothes,
    we wash the clothes,
Dollies' hose, and underclothes,
    On a washing-day in the morning

This is the way we wring the clothes,
    we wring the clothes,
    we wring the clothes,
Everyone knows we wring the clothes
    On a washing-day in the morning.

This is the way we dry the clothes,
    we dry the clothes,
    we dry the clothes.
You don't suppose dolls wear wet clothes
    On a Summer's day in the morning.

And this is the way we wash the clothes,
And wring them out, as you may suppose,
And hang them up, as everyone knows,
    On a washing day in the morning.

PASTORAL

I CANNOT sing of Spring-time
            when the leaves are falling fast,
I cannot sing of Summer before the Winter's past,
Of sweet blue sky and sunshine whilst yellow fogs do last.
    But this, good sir, is what you must do
    When the Printer's Boy is waiting for you.

I cannot sing of violets, of bluebells, lilies light,
When the garden and the forests and the fields are all in white;
I cannot sing of morning when all around is night.
    But then, what will the Publisher do
    And the Printer's Boy who's waiting for you?

I cannot sing a Pastoral, of lambs within the fold,
Of merry, happy childhood
           when my heart is growing old;
How can I tell a new tale
           when all my tales are told?
You must wait for songs of sunshine
           till the skies have ceased to rain,
You must wait for songs of Spring-time
           till the swallows come again;
To sing to skies so cold and grey
           is but to sing in vain.
    All this, good sir, is perfectly true,
    But the Printer's Boy won't wait for you!

SAY "PLEASE."

FAN, come here:
   Make a bow,
There's a dear
   Good bow-wow.

Fido's good,
   And he sees
That he should
   Say "yes, please."

   So must you,
     Fan, my dear,
   Do so too,
     Now, you hear.

"If you please"
   Is polite,
And "thank you,"
   Fan, is right.

   Dinner's here;
     Fido he's
   Waiting, dear,
     Now say "please."

A NEW BOOK.

WHEN I am very big and old,
    I'll write a book all bound in gold.

These are the things of which, I think,
I'll write about in pen and ink.

My dicky bird in his nice cage,
I'll write about him on one page.

I'll tell about my pussy-cat,
Who goes to sleep upon the mat.

Of my new shoes; and dolly too —
I won't forget to 'member you.

        About the flowers that come and go
        In my own garden where they grow.

        The other boys and girls I'll tell
        Of Mother dear, I love so well.

        I'll write a book all bound in gold,
        When I'm a big man five years old.

DAISIES.

"OF all the flowers that are so sweet,"
    Said little Daisy Pringle,
"I love the daisies 'neath my feet
    That grow down in our dingle.

    "In all the world no daisies grow
       Like those in our own dingle;
    But that's because I love them so,
       Said little Daisy Pringle.

    The sweetest Daisy that *I* know
       Is little Daisy Pringle;
    But then, you know, I love her so,
       And she lives in our dingle.

SUPPOSE.

SUPPOSE the Old Woman who lived in a Shoe,
    Had lived in a cottage, she'd know what to do
With her children; she need not have sent them to bed,
But let them play "puss-in-the-corner" instead.
But I fear it's too late—the old woman's dead.

Suppose that Miss Muffet had sat on a chair
Instead of a tuffet, I think that it's fair
To suppose that the spider, who loved curds and whey,
Would have dined off a fly in the usual way,
And so saved Miss Muffet much trouble that day.

And then if Bo-peep kept, instead of her sheep,
Some guinea-pigs, they'd never cause her to weep
For the loss of their tails, for, you see, they don't choose
To wear tails, and so they have nothing to lose
(Indeed, if you offered them tails they'd refuse).

Suppose that we only could manage to see
Each story-book ending up quite happily.
Suppose that the Babes in the Wood didn't die;
And Cock Robin, poor fellow,
    and many more—why,
It would save many tears
    in your dear little eye.

Suppose that your sum
    won't add up, dear; why, then,
Suppose carry one
    and twice five could make ten.
Suppose and suppose
    and suppose, dear, that we
Could change things, how very much
    changed they would be;
But as we can't change them,
    I think we agree
To let them remain as they are,
    don't you see?

THE
BETTER LAND.

SINCE Mother went away, Cissie, since Mother went away,
   The days have been so cold and dark, and we're too sad to play;
So let us go together, Ciss, together hand in hand,
The way that Mother went that day into the better land.

That land is far away, dearie, that land is far away,
Beyond the far tall chimney-tops—beyond the stars, they say;
'Tis a long and toilsome way, dearie, but patience, hand in hand,
Each day will bring us nearer Mother and the better land.

A DONKEY RACE.

" *THIS* is the way we ride a race,
                we ride a race,
                we ride a race,
And really we go at a fearful pace,
        On donkey-back of a morning.

"We each have a donkey what *will* go,
                what *will* go,
                what *will* go,
And the donkeys like it, don't you know,
        On the sands of a Summer morning.

        "*I think I should like to see the race,*
                to see the race,
                to see the race."
        "We fear, dear sir, it's out of the case,
                To show you the race this morning."

        We regret we cannot, for want of space,
        Show you the whole of the donkey race,
        Which really was run at a dreadful pace
                On a Summer's day
                        in the morning.

*W*HAT does my Maudie sing?
 Birdie sweet,
You are sweet, so sweet!
Rest, little feet.
    Rest, rest.
    Your little breast
    Is soft as silk,
    White as milk.
    Coo, coo,
    Means: "I love you,"
    Birdie mine,
You are sweet, so sweet!

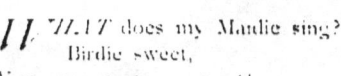

What does my Mother sing?
 Birdie *mine*,
You are sweet, so sweet!
Tired heart, you beat.
    Rest, rest
    On Mother's breast.
    Four years old,
    Heart of gold,
    Eyes blue
    Say: "I love you,"
    Birdie *mine*,
You are sweet, so sweet.

A LAPFUL
OF DAISIES.

HIGH, low, all of a row,
  Down where the daisies and buttercups grow:
    Daisies are sweet
    For Dobbin to eat;
Dobbin's our dear old pony, you know.

  High, low, all in a row,
Down where the clover and meadowsweet grow;
    Swift run the feet;
    Your lapful sweet
Of daisies to dear old Dobbin shall go.

  Here we go, all in a glow,
Down where Dobbin is waiting, we know,
    Isn't it sweet
    Daisies to eat,
Down where the daisies and buttercups grow?

AN UNKNOWN LAND.

AND won't you come this way," said he,
  "Sweet mistress, by my side?
    It isn't very far, you know:
      No harm can us betide;
  Besides, I love you, dear, so well,
    And you can take my hand,
  And we will go together
    To find that unknown land
  Where the sun is always shining,
    And the shores are golden sand."

So with a trustful little smile
  The pretty blue-eyed miss
Just put her tiny hand in his
  And gave the sweetest kiss.
And many a wayside flower they plucked,
  And wandering path they took
By ferny hollow, field, and fen,
  By many a bank and brook,
Seeking their sunny unknown land,
  With eager, hopeful look.

  And now, though golden hair grows grey,
    They still walk side by side.
  The path they tread together
    Leads by the river-side,
  But still no shadow dims their eyes
    As they walk hand in hand,
  And surely they have found at last
    That happy unknown land
  Where the sun is always shining,
    And the shores are golden sand.

THE ORPHAN.

LIE still, my pretty one,
  Lie still and rest;
You shall be snug and warm,
You are quite safe from harm,
  Safe on my breast.

Though you are motherless,
  Though you are lone,
I will be kind to you,
Temper the wind to you,
  Pretty, my own.

Beat not so fearfully,
  Poor little heart,
Danger is far away --
Far as yon star away.
  Why dost thou start?

Lie still, my pretty one,
  Lie still and rest;
You shall no longer roam
You shall be safe at home
  Safe on my breast.

A TEA-PARTY.

THIS sweet little party, consisting of three,
  Have taken their doggie, and gone out to tea.
I would have gone too, but they didn't ask me.

They've teacups and tea-things, of teaspoons a few,
Some real china plates, and a big teapot too,
And a dear little kettle that's nearly brand new.

They've plum-cake and cherries and pears with their tea,
But they've no bread-and-butter that I can see—
They must have forgotten to bring it, these three.

There's no nursie here any bother to make,
There's no one to ask you what you will take,
Or to say: "I think that you've had enough cake."

Good-bye, little party consisting of three!
I wish for you all, though you didn't ask me,
Many happy returns of your Afternoon Tea.

LITTLE ACTS
OF KINDNESS.

LITTLE acts of kindness,
    Like a summer flower,
Brighten many a weary face,
    Soothe a lonely hour.

Hearts are full of sorrow,
    Faces pale and sad;
We can bring them sunshine,
    We can make them glad.

Let us seek to scatter,
    Let us seek to sow
Little seeds of kindness
    Everywhere we go.

MY LITTLE SWEETHEART.

O SHIP, you white-winged seagull,
   Bring home my love to me!
Her face is like a cloudless sky,
   Her hair a Summer sea.
O Ship, you white-winged seagull,
   Bring home my love to me!

O Western Wind, blow softly;
   O Eastern Wind, blow low;
O Happy Sea, your bosom
   Bears my dear love, I know;
And you are haply jealous
   Of her blue eyes, I trow.

And the Western Wind blew softly,
   And the Eastern Wind blew low,
And into my safe haven
   A stately ship they blow;
And this is my dear Sweetheart
   With her blue eyes, I trow.

A LULLABY.

SLEEP, Baby, sleep!
   The wind is driving
         the red, red leaves,
The birds are hiding
         beneath the eaves,
The sun sinks softly to rest.
    Pretty one, sleep, sleep!

    Sleep, Baby, sleep!
The black clouds have
        curtained the eastern sky,
The moon, in a silver sea, sails by,
  And the stars shine out in the west.
    Little one, sleep, sleep!

    Sleep, Baby, sleep!
The night winds murmur across the wold,
The lambkins lie close
        in the shade of the fold,
  Lie close in the mother sheep's breast.
    Pretty one, sleep, sleep!

WHAT WOULD YOU SAY TO THAT?

*I*F facts could rhyme
            with fancies,
And "dog" could rhyme with "rat."
If little you were double you,
        What would you say to that?

If Dolly dressed its mistress.
        The china broke the cat,
If all the sea were made of tea,
        What would you say to that?

If poets lived on verses
        (I don't think they'd grow fat).
If boys were fed on ginger-bread,
        What would you say to that?

If two folk in the parlour
        Should stop for idle chat.
Should faces meet with kisses swe—
        What would you say to *that?*

WONDERS.

"I WONDER," said Miss Ethel,
        "if my lover's on the se
And if his little ship is really
        sailing home to me."

"I wonder too," said Freddy, "if when I am a man
I shall find a Treasure Island: I shall try to if I can."

"I know," said Maud, "the Bogey comes to us when we're not goo
I wonder if he really lives in a great big dark black wood."

"I wonder," said the Baby, "if the stars up in the sky
Are little holes for God to peep down from His Throne on high

"I wonder if the world ends up in the hills so high,
Where the clouds come down and touch the ground and the hi
    tops touch the sky."

"I wonder," said the little mouse, "if you can tell me, please
I wonder if it's really true the moon is made of cheese."

A BOY'S PRAYER.

"PRAY God bless my dear Mamma,
    And please take care of dear Papa;
Let no ill dreams my sleep annoy,
And make Freddy a good boy.
                        Amen."

THE night has come, the day is dead;
Good children all should be abed;
God send sweet dreams into each head,
All the way round the Clo